Grant Allen

The Jaws of Death

A novel

Grant Allen

The Jaws of Death
A novel

ISBN/EAN: 9783337036720

Printed in Europe, USA, Canada, Australia, Japan

Cover: Foto ©Andreas Hilbeck / pixelio.de

More available books at **www.hansebooks.com**

THE JAWS OF DEATH

A NOVEL

BY

GRANT ALLEN

SANS PEUR ET
SANS REPROCHE

L & N

LONDON
JARROLD & SONS
10 AND 11 WARWICK LANE E.C.   1896

CONTENTS.

THE JAWS OF DEATH.

CHAPTER I.

A PIONEER OF COOPER'S PIKE.

"Enjoy the spring of Love and
    Youth,
      To some good angel leave the
      rest ;
      For Time will teach thee soon the
      truth,
      There are no birds in last year's
      nest ! "
LONGFELLOW.

WHY, certainly. A great
many folks ask me what it
was that turned my hair
white. And you don't often
see a young man of my age
with snow-white locks like
these, I'm aware. I con-
sider it a *spécialité*. Well,
it was that awful night at
San Francisco that did it, if

you want to know. I tell you, gentlemen, if ever any fellow was rescued from the jaws of death by the skin of his teeth, it's the individual that now stands before you. But it's a long yarn, and a dry yarn, and it'll take some time to tell it properly. Let's adjourn to the billiard-room, and have it all out over a brandy and soda, since you *will* be inquisitive. I always require a brandy and soda myself when I tell that tale, just to keep my mouth moist; the horror of the thing comes back to me so still, that it somehow seems to dry my blood up.

But first, before I begin to reach the tragedy of it— for you may guess it *was* a tragedy, and no mistake— let me start fair with the story how I came at all, an Englishman born and bred, and one of the Frekes of Devonshire, to go to San Francisco.

8

You've had a cursory look round Cooper's Pike this afternoon in my buggy, and you can see what sort of a city it is nowadays. There isn't another manufacturing town on the Pacific slope that can hold a candle to Cooper's Pike this minute in the matter of industries. We claim to do the biggest trade in hardware of any city in the State, and our population ran out to over seventy thousand souls at the last enumeration. But the Pike was a precious different sort of a place when I first came here, ten years since. A more one-horse affair than it looked then you never saw.

It was a miserable village of a single long street, and low at that, consisting in about equal proportions of a hotel, a dancing-saloon, three American bars, a provision store, a shooting-gallery, and a Chinese laundry. People

PEOPLE

said, those days, it was better
to live in vain than to live
in Cooper's Pike City. The
inhabitants reckoned about
forty men and three women;
and so far as I could see
they didn't appear to have a
single immortal soul among
them. "Hallo!" said I, when
I first set eyes on the town
of Cooper's Pike; "here's a
pretty sort of place indeed
for me to bring Edith to!"

And that reminds me that
I'd better start fair at the
very beginning, and tell you
who I was, and who was
Edith.

Well, I'd come fresh out
from the old country in those
days, like many another
young fellow of good family
and insufficient brains, to
seek my fortune in the
western territories. I'd been
a couple of years a medical
student at Bartholomew's
before I left home; but Bartholomew's and I didn't get
on together, somehow; and

Bartholomew's had the mean-
ness to insinuate it was my
own fault rather than theirs,
for being a lazy young vaga-
bond, and neglecting anatomy
and physiology with impartial
carelessness. Perhaps it was;
for I was never a dab at
books, and I didn't take
enthusiastically to dissect-
ing, either; but anyhow, my
mother went on Bartholo-
mew's side, and shipped me
off to America to shift for
myself on a ranch or something. The dear old lady
meant to do her best for me,
I don't doubt; and so she
did in the end, as I guess
you'll judge if you look
around my residence here;
for we're not what you call
indigent; and by way of
settling me down in life as
a complete rancher — why,
she bought me a small town
lot for a nominal price in
Cooper's Pike City. Cooper's
Pike wasn't then on the
boom; but a land company

in England was doing its best to boom it. She bought it, on paper, at an agency in Pall Mall ; and I, who didn't know a ranch from a ten o' spades in those days—I went readily enough wherever the mater chose to send me. " Honour your father and your mother," was good enough for me ; and, as my mother wished it, I was prepared to run my own ranch undisturbed on a fifty-feet frontage right here in Main Street.

So having nothing to live upon, and no prospects in particular to look forward to in life, I need hardly tell you that the very first thing I did on my way out, on board the *Scythia*, was to fall in love with the prettiest and most delicately nurtured girl in all England.

Her name was Edith Deverel — the Devonshire Deverels, too—and she was going out with her father,

FATHER,

who was in the consular
service, to spread sweetness
and light in Yokohama.

As they were bound for
Japan, *via* San Francisco,
and as I was going in the
same direction as far as
Carson (where I was to
branch off for my property
on the Cooper's Pike trail),
we naturally chummed up
from the very first day we met
on board ; and I've always
noticed that when a young
man and a young woman
chum up together on a
Cunard steamer, you may
smell wedding-cake looming
up indefinitely in the dim
distance. A mixed meta-
phor, is it, sir ? Well,
perhaps it is ; we're not particular about mixing our
liquors, right out here in the
West. As long as we make
ourselves understood, we let
the rest slide. And I fancy
you more or less comprehend
my meaning.

So, to cut a long story

short, and get into the thick
of things at once, as Horace
recommends—you see, I still
retain reminiscences of the
dear old Charterhouse —
before we reached New
York, we were regularly
engaged ; and likely to re-
main so for an indefinite
period.

At the moment, however,
that didn't trouble me much.
I was happy enough in
having induced Edith to be
mine for life ; and the mere
trifling fact that she was to
be mine at Yokohama, while
I was to be hers in the
territory of Nevada, six
thousand miles away, didn't
seem to interfere in the very
least with the depth and
serenity of our youthful
transports. Young people
don't duly appreciate at first
the importance of contiguity
in matters of this sort. They
think you can love one
another equally well in spite
of space-relations ; which, as

Euclid would say, is absurd
and impossible. If I was
one of the Bureau of National
Proverbs, I'd make the
children write at the top of
their copy - books, " Pro-
pinquity is the mother of
intersexual affection."

However, as far as Carson
City we went together very
happily over the Union
Pacific line to our various
destinations. The very name
seemed to give us a fortunate
omen. The Union Pacific
line! Could anything on
earth be more delightful?
Yokohama and Cooper's
Pike united together in the
bond of love and fortnightly
correspondence! We gloated
over the idea, and I almost
fancy I made it the subject
of my muse's first and only
sonnet.

But when I left the cars
at Carson City—yes, sir, I
have got Americanized, some,
in ten years at Cooper's
Pike; I frankly admit it;

the Pacific slope is sur-
prisingly assimilative ; no-
where like it on earth for
absorbtive power—when I
left the cars at Carson City,
I began to feel in a vague
sort of way that perhaps I'd
done rather a mean thing in
asking Edith to throw herself away on a good-for-
nothing emigrant, who hadn't
a prospect in the world or a
red cent to bless himself
with. As I drove across
country on Jim Fletcher's
stage to Cooper's Pike, three
days' journey over a road
which would make an Irish
carman's hair stand on end
with horror, this feeling
gradually deepened upon me.
And when at last I reached
Pike itself, and examined life
near the setting sun, on the
site of Edith's future home,
I felt in a moment I could
never ask that ethereal crea-
ture to come down from the
clouds and partake of hash
daily in a lumber-built shanty.

16

SHANTY.

For there wasn't a stone house anywhere in Cooper's Pike, in those days, nor a house of any sort except right here on Main Street. There wasn't a side walk, or a horse-car, or a respectable woman. The cross streets were staked out to be sure, at regular angles, in very good style ; the company did that ; but only the stakes themselves as yet were visible ; and as the Boys used them for firing at in revolver practice, they tended to deteriorate before the city grew up and obliterated them entirely.

However, I was never one to be daunted by hardships. I set to work at once, with the aid of Joe Ashley, the barman at the saloon, to construct myself a hut on my fifty-feet frontage. It wasn't much of a hut, I allow, for it was built entirely of broken cracker-boxes—I beg your pardon, gentlemen ; I forgot you were from the other side—packing cases for biscuits. I bought them at the grocery store for two days' labour, splitting firewood; and when the hut was built, a neater or more commodious shanty of its sort you never saw; if only it had been watertight, it would have been replete with every modern convenience. But the rain dropping through where the shingles misfitted *did* keep one awake a bit at night sometimes; and I must say the absence of a floor was a distinct disadvantage, whenever one had to sit with one's feet in a puddle. But bless you, you can't expect to have French cookery and lectures on Esoteric Buddhism in a new settlement; you're not fit for Nevada if you can't put up with a little gentle roughing it.

Well, of course I didn't like to worry my old mater

at home with small details
of that sort—she might have
thought I'd catch cold if she
knew I had to lie with the
drip from the roof falling on
to my blanket; and she'd
have had her fears for my
morals, I expect, if she'd
learnt the antecedents of the
only ladies (all three of them
unmarried) then located in
the Cooper's Pike settlement.
So, just to let her down easy,
I put the best face upon it.
I wrote home as cheerfully
about things generally as I
could honestly write. I told
her I'd got myself a neat
small house built on the lot
she'd bought me; that I was
on intimate terms with the
best society of the place;
and that I hoped before long
to find some business open-
ing in the lumbering interest.
And indeed, Joe the barman
was very good society; and
the demand for steady hands
to split firewood and drive
teams to the mines was

regularly increasing with the pan-out of the silver.

For about three months I went on picking up odd jobs here and there, and living from hand to mouth in a way that afforded me lots of fun for my money ; and I also kept on writing to Edith at Yokohama, assuring her always of my undying affection, and of the absolute impossibility of its ever assuming a more tangible shape than that afforded by a long fortnightly letter. But at the end of three months, as I was washing out molasses barrels one day (at twenty cents an hour) for my friend at the grocery store, up comes the stage from Carson City, and Jim Fletcher jumps off and steps along quite important-like — "Howard Freke, Esquire," says he, with a polite bow, "I've got a letter for you, sir. Boys, this is an event that inaugurates a new era. First

United States mail that ever entered Cooper's Pike City!"

Naturally, the Boys all crowded round me; and naturally, too, they shook my hands, and congratulated me and themselves warmly upon this auspicious occurrence. They felt it was an occasion for glasses all round; and on the strength of my letter, I treated the company. After that, I retired to my own hut, to read the mater's letter in peace and quietness.

Well, I don't want to say anything disrespectful about my mother, but I must confess the contents of that first communication from home, read in the gloom of my biscuit-box hut, did rather amuse me. My mother hoped I was very particular what society I picked up with, and that I attended Divine service twice regularly on Sundays. (The nearest church, those days, was three days off, you

must recollect, at Carson
City.) She hoped also I
had furnished my house
quietly and inexpensively,
and had been very careful
about sanitary arrangements,
and gone in for nice light
cheerful papers. She hoped
I would look after the house-
keeping accounts with rigour,
and not let the cook buy
fresh meat for stock, which
could be made every bit as
good from bones, and so
forth. She was surprised I
had got on so well at the
lumbering in so short a
time; but she knew men got
good appointments easily in
the far West; and she was
always sure I'd do really
well, like a trueborn Freke,
if once I put my heart
thoroughly into it. And
then came the chief point
of all in the whole letter:
"As I wish to mark my
pleasure at your earnest
desire to help yourself in
your new home, and as I

I

think it highly desirable you should as far as possible keep up your music—you play so nicely, and musical evenings are such a resource to young men away from home—I have decided to contribute to the furnishing of your house "—well, what do you think, gentlemen ?—" a new grand piano."

When I came to that, all alone among my biscuit-boxes, I burst out laughing. Why, my whole hut itself wasn't big enough for the piano even to stand in !

As soon as I'd finished the letter, I went out, rather shamefaced, to see the Boys again. I didn't dare to tell them the story about the piano. I knew how they'd laugh at me and at the dear old mater. But I took it for granted the confounded thing would never get further than Carson City at the very outside. The bare idea of bringing it right through

to the Pike was just too
ridiculous!

The dear old mater had
precious little notion what
sort of place the Pike was,
if she thought a piano would
be much in demand there.

CHAPTER II.

"Be still, sad heart! and cease re-
     pining;
   Behind the clouds is the sun still
     shining;
   Thy fate is the common fate of all,
   Into each life some rain must fall,
     Some days must be dark and
       dreary."
                        LONGFELLOW.

ABOUT a week later I was
loafing around at the corner
by the Columbia Saloon,
waiting for any odd job that
might happen to turn up—
they wanted extra hands
sometimes at the crushing-
works if the ore was rich,
and I was never too proud
to do anything useful—when
all of a sudden I heard a
thundering noise down the
street in the direction of the

25   D

grocery store; a noise as if heaven and earth were coming together, as Chicken-picken says in the good old nursery book. The Boys had all turned out *en masse*, and were cheering like mad, and waving their hands, and laughing as I never saw human beings laugh in this world before, outside a lunatic asylum.

And something or other big was obstructing the roadway.

"What's up?" I called out to Joe Ashley, the bartender, who was standing down street a bit, looking after the cooperage.

"Dunno," Joe answered, shading his eyes with his hand and staring straight in front of him. "Seems like a box coming up the road. The darnedest big box that ever came into the Pike, I should say, by the look of it. There's six mules to draw it; six mules, Indian

26

file. Well, this is civilization, an' no mistake. The other day we landed a United States mail; and now, bless me, if this ain't a cottage grand, imported into the settlement!"

"A *what?*" I cried, growing pale with fright; for I had a sort of presentiment all at once of the trouble before me.

"A cottage grand!" says Joe. "A pianny, don't you catch on? The Boys must be preparing a surprise for old Wesley. Well, this *is* civilization and no mistake. To think I should live to see a cottage grand arriving in triumph, with six mules in single file, into the streets of Cooper's Pike City."

He said "streets" in the plural from pure force of habit, I reckon, for there was only the one, bar the stakes and the bullet-holes.

Well, I did just tremble when I knew what it was.

WAS.

I set out for the front, as
you can readily conjecture,
with all my legs, and never
drew rein, metaphorically
speaking, till I came right
up to the spot where the
Boys were cavorting, cheering, and hooraying.

" Hello, Freke ! " they
cried out, as I ran up to
them breathless. " Here's
a little present your girl's
been sending you from Old
England, most likely. A
small souvenir for you to
wear around your neck in a
locket. It's taken five days
to come across by the trail
from Carson City."

You can just judge of my
chagrin, gentlemen, when I
looked at that huge, big,
lumbering box, and read on
the side in plain English
letters, " From Broadwood
and Co., London. Piano,
with care. This side up.
To be kept dry. Howard
Freke, Esq., Main Street,
Cooper's Pike, Nevada."

28

I could have thrown myself under the wheels with rage and shame. How on earth could the mater ever have made such a fool of me?

"Where do you wish it delivered, mister?" the driver in charge asked me, with a broad grin on his stupid mug.

"Delivered!" I cried, fuming. "The Lord knows where. Deliver it where you like, and then go home. There isn't a private house in the Pike big enough to hold it."

"Then what are we to do with it?" says the driver, quite jauntily.

"Do with it?" says I. "Why, plump it down right here! I guess it won't much matter obstructing the traffic."

"Well, there's a trifle to pay on it, for freight and customs duty," says the driver, with a smile, pulling out a Union Pacific Railroad Company's form. "Let's

see. This is it. Howard
Freke, Cooper's Pike City:
to collect—three hundred
and forty-seven dollars."

I sat down on the ground
in blank despair. I tore my
hair. I almost cried in my
agony. Three hundred and
forty-seven dollars, indeed !
And I hadn't three hundred
and forty cents to my blessed
name. This was worse than
beggary. It was bankruptcy,
insolvency, disgrace, ruin !

"I haven't got it !" I cried.
" Take the nasty thing back.
It isn't for me. I don't want
your piano. It must be for
another gentleman of the
same name. You may return
it, post free, by the next
delivery, this side up, to
Broadwood and Company,
London."

Well, the Boys began to
see I was really riled, and
that the affair was beginning
to take a serious turn for
me. The Boys are a genuine
good-natured lot, when one

comes to know them ; and I fancy they'd somehow taken a sort of liking to me, because I was young and unsophisticated, and knew a trifle about dressing wounds, and could sing them a sentimental song in the evenings sometimes, when they were in the right mood, and wrote letters home for some of the rougher lot who couldn't write themselves, to their wives or sweethearts. You mayn't believe it, gentlemen, but Cooper's Pike was so rough in those days, that even a rejected medical student was a sort of a kind of civilizing element. It was Joe the bar-tender who began it. "Boys," said he, "it ain't right the burden of the first pianny that ever came into Cooper's Pike City should fall on the shoulders of a single green youngster ; especially as he don't happen to have the costs of freight lying handy in his pocket,

which is an accident that
may happen to any gentle-
man any day, in a fresh
community. Now, this is
an opportunity that may not
again occur. We've got a
pianny to-day actually in our
midst; and we've a talented
fellow-citizen, Howard Freke,
of England, who knows how
to play on it. What I pro-
pose is this, that we get up
a subscription to pay for the
freight on the instrument,
and that we put it in the
saloon, where Howard Freke
can discourse sweet music to
us while we take our liquor,
evenings. Those who are
in favour of this notion, put
their dollars in the hat; those
who are against it, stand
aside in a row, so that we
may know which of the in-
habitants are darned eastern
skunks and which are generous, free-handed, Nevadan
gentlemen."

Well, the Boys caught
on to it with regular mining

enthusiasm. Joe dropped
in a dollar, just to start the
game, as it were; and Wesley Smith, the saloon-keeper,
followed with ten, for he saw
it meant good business for
the liquor-trade interest. In
a quarter of an hour, Joe's
idea had panned out rich;
they'd subscribed enough to
discharge that impossible
debt, as it seemed to me
at first; and they'd handed
over the money in due form
to the Union Pacific driver.
Then they all joined hands,
and escorted the piano home
to the saloon, where it was
solemnly opened with proper
celebration, and installed in
the place of honour over
against the fireplace. Nothing would do for the Boys
after that but I must sit
down then and there and
play them "Hail, Columbia."
I didn't know the score, to
speak of, but the Boys are
never very particular about
an accompaniment; and

when I'd finished, they en-
cored it like mad ; and then
I gave them " God save the
Queen," by way of making
an international event of it.
After that, they stood drinks
all round to the driver and
his men, and voted a feed
of corn to the mules, and
solemnly declared the piano
public property, for the benefit of the citizens of Cooper's
Pike City.

At the end of it all, just
as the fun of the joke was
beginning to subside, and
the company was half-in-
clined to disperse to its
own huts, a sudden thought
struck Joe, the bar-tender.

" Why, Boys," he called
out, standing on a chair to
make himself heard, " it just
occurs to me, we've never
pay for this pianny itself at
all. All we've done is to
pay the freight of it. We
ought to get up another
subscription to buy the instrument from our talented

friend Freke, and present it in perpetuity to this city. I reckon you wouldn't get a pianny like that for a cent less than three hundred dollars."

I confess I'd never thought of that point of view myself. I was so precious glad to have got out of my scrape that the value of the piano, as an article of merchandise, never even occurred to me.

"Oh, don't mind the cost," said I, getting up on another chair in my turn, and growing rather red. "That's all right. So far as the original price of the thing's concerned, I don't mind making a free gift of it to the city."

It was my first free gift to the Pike, and I felt rather proud of it.

The Boys, however, were too generous to take it. They wanted to send round the hat again, and subscribe for the purchase. Still, I was sort of ashamed to receive their cash, after all their kindness; so at the end of ten minutes' talk, we effected a compromise. Wesley Smith, the saloon-keeper, had got a corner lot—same where the Central Gas Office stands to-day; and he proposed to throw it in with a month's board as payment in full for the grand piano. I didn't want to haggle, as between gentlemen, so I accepted the offer. I became the owner before night of that corner lot, with the papers all duly signed, sealed, and delivered; and that was the beginning, gentlemen, of the Cooper's Pike manufacturing interest.

Yes, sir, that's so; you've not been misinformed. It was I that gave the San Quentin Park to the city, and that presented the Free Public Library and Museum to the Mechanics' Institute. Oh no, that's nothing. I don't look upon it as generosity at all; I call it simple justice. You see, it was all luck that started me in life; I had no more right to it than anybody else, by nature; and I hold it all now in trust for society. Whatever I give ain't exactly what you can call a free gift, is it? It's rather in the nature of a sort of restitution, don't you see? a kind of rendering to Cæsar the things that are Cæsar's— giving back the people their own, for their own sole use and benefit.

CHAPTER III.

THE CORNER LOT.

"We live in deeds, not years; in
    thoughts, not breaths,
  In feelings, not in figures on the
    dial.
  We should count time by heart-
    throbs.   He most lives
  Who thinks most, feels the noblest,
    acts the best."
                    PHILIP BAILEY.

You don't see what that
corner lot had to do with
the manufacturing interest
in the city, don't you? Well,
that was rather a curious
little incident, too. It's worth
telling; and it's part of the
same story.   It just came
about this way, pretty much,
I take it.

When the piano was safely
housed and set up in the
Columbia   Saloon,   under

UNDER

Wes. Smith's charge, but as
public property, the Boys
decided that I ought at least
to retain the packing-case.
A lot of good timber like
that, ready shaped and
planed, was worth something
on a Pike, I can tell you.
And as I'd been rather down
on my luck lately, and the
Boys liked me because I
could play them a lively tune,
evenings, and looked after
the two men that were hurt
when the roof fell, they
volunteered to help me
build a better hut out of it,
on that corner lot of three
and a half acres. Wesley
Smith bought the other lot
off me for an extension of
the saloon to hold the piano ;
and the Boys undertook to
raise me a house where the
rain wouldn't drip through,
and to pave it well with
rubble from the diggings.

Why, yes, we built the
house ; and though it's me
that says it, as oughtn't to

say it, a tidier hut you never saw in any new diggings. We were all rather proud of that hut, as a specimen of Nevadan architecture. The evening it was finished, I invited as many of the Boys as could get in to partake of square drinks all round, on the strength of my week's work as a help at the crushing. The Boys turned up, you may be sure, in full force, and my one room was packed as tight as the four walls could hold, so that some of us actually bulged out of the window. But we had a high old time of it for all that, singing and jollifying, till the room got so hot we could hardly stand it.

" There's a precious queer smell in this hut," one of the Boys said at last, sniffing up a little high-toned; " seems to me, Freke, there must be something or other gone wrong with your main drainage."

Well, I laughed at that, for, of course, drainage of any sort was an idea we hadn't struck as yet on the Pike; but, just to make things pleasant, and keep up the joke, I answered naturally, "No, it isn't drains, Pete; it's a leakage in the gas-pipes you smell, I fancy."

"By George!" says Pete, sniffing the air again, "now you come to say the word, I believe it *is* gas I smell. The gas is most certainly escaping somewhere."

As he spoke, every man Jack of us held his nose in the air, and sniffed instinctively after him. I can see it now: such a picture of aristocratic high-sniffing noses, all poised in a row, prospecting around, and all critically investigating, you never saw in your born days. It was a thing to remember. And well may I remember it. Then we all of us turned, and looked at one another with blank faces of surprise. There was no denying it. We couldn't say what tricks the Boys might have been playing us. But there, in that one-horse town of cheap kerosene lamps, and dear at that, as clear as the human nose could tell us, I assure you, gentlemen, the gas was escaping.

Joe Ashley, the bar-tender, was the first to speak. "Yes, sir. It's gas, and no mistake," he said, looking scared, for we all of us felt there was something mysterious and just a wee bit uncanny about it.

" The march of intellect's something reeley surprising," Pete put in, looking around. " Last week it was a pianny. The week afore, it was mails. This week, it's gas-works."

But most of us were a good deal too thunderstruck by that time for joking. We took the thing seriously.

42

SERIOUSLY.

You see, in those days, we were hardly prepared for miracles to take place in the nineteenth century. We'd been taught that the age of miracles was past. I went down on my hands and knees, and began to examine the floor narrowly, having a vague sort of notion, don't you understand, that the gas-pipes would naturally run underground, as they always do in civilized countries. In a minute, sure enough, I detected the leak. A tiny jet of gas was forcing itself up through a hole in the floor, as distinct as ever you smelt a leakage of gas in a London lodging-house.

I struck a match, and lighted the jet. It burnt clear and beautiful, with a full bright flame, as fine as ever you saw in a London burner.

We looked at one another, and never said a word. When I read in Keats afterwards about Cortez and his men, "Silent, upon a peak in Darien," it brought back to me exactly how we all looked at one another at the moment of that discovery.

We'd none of us ever heard of natural gas before : it was a new thing then ; but in a second, we all took in the importance of the find. We'd struck it rich ; of that we felt certain. The Boys began prodding with knives and sticks all over the floor, and poking a match to the jets ; and wherever they prodded the gas came out, a burst of it at once, till the hut was a perfect Fourth of July illumination. The fact was, all that lot, and many another lot in Cooper's Pike, was a natural gas-reservoir. But nobody'd happened to build before on one of the spots where the gas oozed out ; and as long as it oozed in the open air, it was so slight a quantity, for the most part, that you never perceived it. If it hadn't been for the accident of my sticking my hut above a small vent, and filling my room so full of people that night that we got half suffocated, I don't suppose the gas would ever have been discovered, and Cooper's Pike would still be a town of some two hundred inhabitants.

As it was, however, we rose to the situation. We began prospecting at once. We found the best outlets were on my corner lot, though there were others in other parts of the city almost as good; and before the week was out we had to exploit them. Nothing like it was ever seen even here in the west. The capital was subscribed like water, and in rather less than no time, the Cooper's Pike Natural Gas Supply Association, of which I am president, was ready

to supply families or com-
mercial firms with gas in
any quantities at reasonable
rates; for cooking, lighting,
house-warming, smelting,
engineering, mining, and
manufacturing purposes. So
rapid a revolution you never
saw. In three months, our
population numbered five
thousand souls, and Main
Street had already the airs
and graces of a fashionable
city.

You see, we made the
gas do just everything. It
does just everything still. It
lights the house; it cooks the
dinner; it warms the parlour;
it turns the mill; it heats
the engine-boiler; it crushes
the ore; it works the factory;
and it runs the mayor and
town council bodily. There's
nothing on earth done in
this city to-day but, if you
look into it closely, the
natural gas does it. We
base ourselves entirely on
natural gas. If the gas were

to go out, we'd go out like a candle. The city arms are three gas-taps, proper, on a field, vert; and the motto runs, "With it, we stand; without it, we totter."

So, after all, I owed everything in the end to my dear old mater's blunder about the grand piano. If it hadn't been for that, I should never have owned the corner lot, and never have become president of the Cooper's Pike Natural Gas Supply Association.

Of course I grew to be rich, western fashion, right off. Without an effort of my own, the money began to tumble in bewilderingly. That's why I say I owe it all to the public. Not but what I manage to live comfortably on it myself too. I allow myself a trifle for the trouble of management. I bought a new lot, right here where we sit, and fixed up a house on it—not the one

47

you see, but its respectable predecessor; for naturally I've gone on getting richer and richer ever since, as the city developed. Still, even the first house was a very convenient one, and I found myself at once a person of great importance in Nevada generally.

The next twelve months were a time of wonders. It isn't often, even on the Pacific slope, that a city has grown up by magic like this one. But here, you see, we had the gas laid on to do the work for us automatically, and all we needed was the hands and brains to guide and direct it. The gas quarried the stone for us, and worked the drills, and hoisted the cranes, and drove the traction engines; and within the year, Main Street had a frontage of fine stone-built stores, and the stakes at the side had developed by a sort of Arabian Nights method into broad avenues of handsome residences fit for respectable and cultured families. There was society in the Pike, now, there was positively society. Ladies with children drove in their own buggies down the new-made roads. A railroad connected us with Carson City, and another joined the North California line by Santander Junction. There was every convenience and comfort of life, except civilized fields and farms about us. And I was myself the richest man, by a long chalk, in the whole community. I bossed the Pike; that's the long and short of it.

One little event happened, however, before I made my journey to San Francisco—the journey that turned my hair white—which I think I ought to tell you about, because it has some bearing, in a way, upon the rest of my story. One day, about

six weeks after the discovery
of gas, while I was up to my
eyes in business, arranging
for the laying down of our
main supply pipes—for we
began from the very first on
the large scale with the
definite idea that Cooper's
Pike was to be a live city—
who should break into my
office but Joe Ashley, the
bar-tender, his eyes blood-
shot, his cheeks pale, and
his whole face looking very
much as if he'd made a night
of it, the evening before, to
very bad purpose. The poor
fellow seemed almost as if
he would burst out crying
before my very face.

"Hallo, Joe," says I;
"why, what on earth's the
matter, man?"

"Drink, Mr. Freke, sir,"
says he. "Drink. Drink.
Drink. That's just about
the name of it."

"How so?" I asked,
sympathizing, for I was sorry
for Joe.

"Well, I met a few friends at the saloon last night," Joe said, making a clean breast of it, and looking very penitent. "And I got precious lively. But that's not the worst of it. One of them friends must have been a bad lot, for there's fifty dollars missing from the till this morning; I don't know how; and I've got the sack; and I'm off to Frisco."

"Fifty dollars," I said, pulling out my purse. "Now, Joe, you can't go and leave the till fifty dollars short, can you? Take this, old fellow, and settle up with the governor," says I, "and then come back and have dinner with me, and we'll talk things over."

For Joe was a very good fellow at bottom, in spite of his small failing; and I could never forget it was he who'd laid the foundation of my own fortunes, by getting up the subscription to pay the piano freight.

51

Well, off Joe went, taking
his money like a man—it
isn't every one that knows
how to accept a favour
gracefully, I can tell you—
and by-and-by he came
back and talked things over;
and I spoke to him like a
father about going to San
Francisco. You've no idea
what a lot of moral dignity I
developed all at once, on the
strength of being president
of the Natural Gas Supply
Association. You see, people always think there's something extremely moral in the
possession of capital. Joe
listened to my preaching as
if I'd been twenty years his
senior, instead of being a
young fellow just out of his
teens. "And now, Joe," I
said, "before you go from
this, you've just got to sign
a little paper for me, if you
please, will you?"

"What is it?" said Joe,
looking at it rather hard.
" Note of hand for fifty?"

FIFTY

"No, no," says I. "Note of hand be blowed! Not that, my friend. Total abstinence pledge for three years certain."

"Will you sign it yourself?" says Joe, drawing back.

"If *you* will," I answered. And I took up a pen, and signed right there. And for three years, gentlemen, just for the sake of example, never a drop of liquor passed my teeth, I can promise you.

"Well, I ain't going to be licked by a boy like you," Joe said, examining my signature with a sort of admiring interest. "You're a plucky one, you are. If *you* can stand the chaff you'll get from the Boys, why, I ought to be able to stand it, I reckon. Here goes," said Joe; and he took up the pen; and for three years after that, you may be sure, he never touched another glass of old Bourbon.

53

BOURBON.

"Now, if you go to San Francisco," I said, putting on a sort of patronizing air, "don't you know, you'll want a trifle to start you in life. You're a good fellow, Joe, and you did me a good turn when I needed one badly. There's two hundred dollars, United States gold. You keep that safe. And mind, when it's gone, if you can't get work, there's plenty more any day where that lot came from."

For the natural gas had worked such an instantaneous revolution in my financial position that a couple of hundred dollars was less to me than twenty cents would have been six weeks before, you may be sure. And I rather liked parading my new-made wealth to Joe, I fancy.

Joe looked at it twice, and then he looked at me. "Mr. Freke," he said, "you're a brick, you are. I'll never touch another drop again, as long as I live; and I'll work like a horse till I've paid you back this. And if ever there's anything I can do to help you, you count on me, sir, and I'll try my best for you."

And sure enough, Joe was as good as his word. He went down to San Francisco, and there he got employment (partly by the aid of a recommendation from me, for, you see, I was beginning to be a somebody on the Pacific slope already), as a clerk in the Pacific Steam Navigation Company's service. And before three months were out, he'd sent me back the two hundred and fifty dollars, United States gold, never having had occasion to touch the two hundred I lent him at all, and having saved the fifty out of his weekly wages. I call that most honourable of Joe Ashley, gentlemen.

CHAPTER IV.

TO SAN FRANCISCO.

"Whene'er a noble deed is wrought,
Whene'er is spoken a noble thought,
Our hearts, in glad surprise
To higher levels rise."
LONGFELLOW.

How about Edith, do you
say, meanwhile? Well, gentlemen, I didn't like to drag in
a lady's name more than I
could help in a billiard-room
conversation; but if you ask
me point-blank, and you *will*
have the truth about it, why,
I don't mind confessing to
you that all this time I'd
been writing by every Pacific
mail, as regular as clockwork, to Edith Deverel, and
keeping as straight, for
Edith's sake, as any young

fellow can hope to do on a
new mining station. The
means of grace aren't largely
developed, as a rule, in a
Pacific settlement. I saw
a good deal of the Boys, of
course, but as far as I could,
I held myself aloof from
drink or play; and after I
signed the pledge, to en-
courage poor Joe, why, I
kept up the dignity of President of the Gas Association
by never going near the
Columbia Saloon at all, by
day or by night, and by
putting on my best London
clothes every Sunday morning, which was the nearest
approach to Divine service
we could manage at the
Pike, till the first Methodist
minister came over from
Carson to run a congrega-
tion. I don't want to talk
sentiment, that's not my line;
but if you think there was
ever a minute of the day
when Edith was out of my
mind, or when thoughts of

what Edith would have wished me to do didn't influence my conduct, why, all I can say is, you've got a less vivid recollection than I have of what sort of a chap I was when I first set up to run the Cooper's Pike Natural Gas Association.

It was a full year, however, before I thought we'd got things ship-shape enough at the Pike to make it possible for me to ask such a lady as Edith to come over as an elevating and refining influence on Nevadan society. At the end of that time, there were several high-toned families settled in the City whom I wouldn't be ashamed to introduce to my wife; and the side-walks were beginning to be fit for the sole of Edith's foot to tread upon. So I wrote and asked her if she'd redeem her pledge, and make me a long sight happier than I could possibly tell her (without

58

exceeding half an ounce) in a twenty-five cent letter. In order to explain things a bit at the same time, I also wrote to her respected papa, informing him that I was now the president of the Cooper's Pike Natural Gas Association, and that if he wanted anything reasonable in the way of settlements, my solicitor would be glad to arrange matters with him on what I trusted would be a mutually satisfactory basis.

Edith herself never hesitated for a moment; I knew she wouldn't; and what was odder still, her papa accepted my financial proposals in the same liberal spirit in which they were intended. I took it kindly of him that he was willing to entrust me with Edith.

So I arranged that my bride was to come over in the next Pacific Steam Navigation Company's packet from Yokohama for San

Francisco; and I determined
to go down to the Golden
Gate myself to meet her in
port on her first arrival. It
was agreed that she should
go, immediately she landed,
to the house of a lady in San
Francisco who knew her
father; and from there she
was to be married at the
earliest possible date, at the
First Episcopal Church in
Madison Street, and go up
country with me straight to
her new location.

Two days before the
vessel was due in port, I
started off by our new rail-
way line *via* Carson City, *en
route* for the Californian
capital.

Now, although we were
in daily business communication with the coast, I had
never myself been in San
Francisco before; and it was
a real treat to me, I can tell
you, after eighteen months
of bustle and hurry in our
mushroom Pike, with its

cranes and its derricks, to
find myself in a civilized
town once more, and to feel
I was again in touch with
old-world culture. So to
fill up the time before Edith
arrived, I began to hunt
about over the sights of the
city.

The first thing I did, however, on arriving at the
Palace Hotel, where I put
up my traps, was to go down
to the Pacific Steam Navigation Company's bureau to
have a chat with Joe Ashley,
the former bar-tender.

Such a respectable man as
Joe'd developed into, under
the joint influence of tee-
totalism and the San Francisco air, you'd hardly ima-
gine unless you could have
seen him. I tell you, that
man wore a black coat, and
was courting a young lady
in an up-town book-store
who'd have done credit at
the head of any merchant's
table on the Pacific sea-

board. It did my heart good to see how nicely he was prospering.

Joe gave my hand such a wring as would have made a good many Englishmen cry out ; but I knew it was well meant, and I thanked him with tears of gratitude in my eyes. Perhaps they weren't altogether gratitude either ; I'm not quite clear about that ; but anyhow they were tears, and that's the main thing, isn't it? He told me the *Sacramento*, that Edith was coming by, claimed to be the fastest steamer on the Japan line, and she might be in, per- haps, that very evening. Or perhaps she mightn't. But she'd be telegraphed up, anyhow, four hours in ad- vance, from the Farallone Islands, where they always signal all approaching vessels. As soon as ever the tele- gram announcing that she'd passed the lighthouse came safe to hand, Joe promised to send a messenger up to my hotel right away with the news, so that I'd have ample time to put on my store clothes, and come down and meet Edith.

That night I went out and had a peep at China Town. I went the usual round of the Chinese Theatre, and the gambling hells, and the hideous dens where the yellow men poison themselves with fumes of opium. But I won't describe them all; they've nothing particular to do with my story. For it wasn't that night that turned my hair grey; not so bad as that; it was the night after. It takes more than China Town, a good deal, to turn my hair white, I can promise you that; though China Town's enough to make it stand on end, if you've never been there. I may be prejudiced, but I don't know how it is,

I never do take to the Chinese somehow.

However, I never went to bed that night. I was too much on the look-out for Edith's arrival. Every hour, I expected to receive a note from Joe Ashley announcing that the *Sacramento* was now in sight; so even after I got home from that horrible sink of filth and iniquity, I sat and read, dozing at times in my chair, and strolling out now and again into the well-lighted streets, just to keep myself from dropping off and forgetting about the steamer.

It was a tedious night, and I was tired with travelling.

Morning dawned at last, and no news of the *Sacramento*. About eight o'clock, after a hasty breakfast, I went down to the bureau and saw Joe once more. He told me there was now no chance of the ship coming alongside before noon at the earliest, so I might go out again and spend the morning, if I liked, in seeing the sights of San Francisco.

Once or twice in the course of the day I called in again at the office, but always with the same stereotyped result : " *Sacramento* not yet telegraphed from the Farallone Islands. At least four hours before she arrives in harbour."

To get rid of the day, therefore, I went a regular round of the San Francisco lions. I drove through the Golden Gate Park; I walked in the Plaza ; I inspected the University ; I tramped along miles of church aisles of every denomination, till I was footsore and weary with my needless exertions. In the afternoon, I hired a hack, and went down for an excursion by a fine boulevard to the Cliff House, where I sat on the verandah and

watched the sea-lions on
Seal Rock, basking in the
sun, or wriggling over the
crags with their discordant
barks, right in front of the
seats in that fashionable
restaurant. But all these
sights gave me very little
satisfaction. By four o'clock
I was back in Market Street
again, only to receive that
one invariable answer: *Sacramento* not yet cabled; call
again for news in three or
four hours."

"What else is there," I
said to Joe, with a despairing yawn, for I was beginning to get tired, "worth a
fellow's going to see in this
great overgrown city?"

"Well, I guess," said Joe,
"there ain't anything much,
now you've done China
Town, and gone through the
Parks; but you might put
in an hour, perhaps, at our
Madame Tussaud's."

"What! you don't mean
to say," I cried, "there's a

Madame Tussaud's here in San Francisco?"

"Well, that ain't exactly its official name," Joe answered: "we only call it that for short, don't you see? Its regular title is the Central Metropolitan Californian Plastographic Museum, for blending amusement and instruction in the education of the masses."

"That's a good word, Plastographic," I said, "if it's in the right place, of course; but whereabouts does the Metropolitan Californian Museum hang out?"

"Corner of Washington and Pacific," says Joe: "eight blocks down. You can't miss your way, and the poster at the door's as big as the City Hall, almost."

"What's the damage?" said I.

"A quarter," said Joe; "and extra for the murderers. But there's a guillotine there that's real fine for the money."

Well, I never was what you could call an enthusiastic devotee of waxworks at any time; they don't come up to my idea of art, like the Romneys in my grandfather's dining-room in Devonshire; and I was tired enough now not to go out of my way if Mont Blanc, Niagara Falls, the Piazza of St. Marks, and the Karnak Temples, had all been on view at once round the nearest corner; but somehow, I felt as if I *must* do something by way of working off my suppressed excitement; so just to pass the time, I took the next street car that came along, and dropped myself down corner of Washington and Pacific, as Joe directed.

The San Francisco Madame Tussaud's was absurdly like the dear old exhibition that used to hang out in Baker Street when I

I was in London (I'm told it's been moved since, with the progress of thought in the old country, to the Marylebone Road—ah, dear, what changes!)—of course with a distinct American flavour thrown in as well; George Washington, and Henry Clay, and the Secretary of the Treasury shaking hands with the President, as a set-off to the late Emperor of the French in his coronation robes, and the Royal Family playing hunt-the-slipper in the drawing-room at Windsor — but on the whole about as much alike in its main features as you expect everything to be nowadays all the world over. There was a Chamber of Horrors, too, as Joe had told me, for which you paid an extra quarter; and there you could see Junius Brutus Booth, in the act of assassinating Abraham Lincoln; as well as Guiteau on trial for his life, after shooting a pasty-faced Garfield in wax at the other end of the raised exhibition platform. There was the usual display of intelligent poisoners, and rascally doctors, and ladies who had anticipated their husband's life - policies, and gentlemen who being unable to marry a couple of wives abreast, had tried to manage it single file by getting off with the old love and on with the new by the agency of a gentle dose of arsenic or antimony. Altogether, a rather depressing spectacle for a man who'd been up in China Town all the night before, and was just waiting for his bride to arrive by steamer from Yokohama.

The most interesting feature in the entire exhibition, however, was the attendant or demonstrator, who accompanied visitors round the Chamber of

Horrors, and explained the
various groups, their crimes
and punishments, with pro-
found gusto. He was a
connoisseur in modes of
death, and his graphic de-
scriptions would have made
the fortune of any penny
dreadful. But what gave
him novelty was the fact
that he was a Chinaman, a
genuine Celestial in a yellow
silk robe and a long pigtail;
and that he descanted on the
nature and deeds of the
various criminals with perfect
assurance in the most lovely
dialect of pigeon English.
At first, he merely amused
and interested me, that man;
I took him as a study of
Oriental character; I had no
idea how soon he was to
interweave himself in fixed
colours into the most awful
incident in my whole career.
Well, yes, gentlemen, you're
about right there. I'm
coming at last in this long
yarn of mine to what it

IT

actually was that turned my
hair white.

And you aren't far wrong
when you say that that
yellow-faced Mongolian had
a good deal to do with it.

CHAPTER V.

"The voyage through life is various
    found.
  The wind is seldom fair;
Though to the straits of pleasure
    bound,
  Too oft we touch at care.
Impervious danger we explore;
  False friends, some faithless she:
Pirates and sharks are found ashore
  As often as at sea."
                        DIBDIN.

HE was a wonderful chap, that Chinaman, and he spoke a wonderful lingo. "Here see Mista Guiteau, Melican gentleman, allee samee like him shoot Plesident Gahfield with loaded levolver at Depôt of Baltimoree and Potomah Lailway. Plesident stand at ease on platform,

73 K

allee likee so; Guiteau comee up, dlaw first-chop pistol; shootee Plesident. Plesident fallee; plenty blood jump out; blood flow down likee water on platform!" Then he smiled a broad smile of supreme content. He leered at the victim. The contemplation of the shot, and the wax blood on the floor, seemed to afford to his mind the supremest satisfaction. I may be prejudiced, but as I said just now, I never did care for these yellow-faced Chinamen.

He would pass on to the next. "Here Missee Bland, Melican lady, poison joss-pigeon man," that's China-Town for a parson, you know; "because he no love her allee samee like she love him—no want to marry her. That not good murder. No use for waxwork. No makee blood. Not muchee for see. Good waxwork murder makee much blood. Fall

out on floor. Melican gentleman likee see plenty blood
when he come visit wax-
work. So much more blood,
so much more Melican
gentleman give cash to
Chinaman."

He was about right as to
the prevailing taste, I don't
doubt; but the stolid, cold-
blooded, Celestial way in
which he gloated over it all
was something truly ridiculous, and yet awful too. I
followed him about just for
the mere curiosity of hear-
ing how he regarded things.
He was a study in character,
and as such he interested
me.

But the thing in the whole
exhibition that seemed to
afford him the profoundest
delight was the inevitable
working-model of a French
guillotine. So fine and so
realistic a guillotine I had
never seen before. On
its block lay a waxwork
gentleman in eighteenth-

75

century dress, supposed to represent King Louis the Sixteenth, in the very act of having his head cut off. Nothing could be more ingenious than the working of this model. The head was joined to the shoulders by a coat of wax; and if the party in the chamber chose to subscribe five dollars between them, they could see the king actually decapitated before their very eyes for that trifle. The money was soon raised, and then the Chinaman, with infinite glee, proceeded to draw the bolt, and let the axe fall on the unfortunate monarch. I never in my life saw anything more hideous. "Why, there's blood in it!" I cried. Medical student as I had been, the horrible realism of the thing fairly took my breath away.

Li Sing smiled. "Yes, leal blood," he answered. "Plenty blood spurt out,

allee samee likee Li Sing
leally cut him head off."

And then he explained it
to me. The head, neck, and
trunk, it seemed, were filled
with blood, real bullock's
blood, "put in flesh every
morning;" it was Li Sing's
business to fill it again, and
remake the neck with wax
after every performance.
When the axe fell, it cut
the head off clean, and at
the same time touched pro-
jecting springs on either
side, which released the im-
prisoned blood by atmos-
pheric pressure. The effect
was ghastly and life-like in
the extreme—or, perhaps, I
ought rather to have said
death-like. You could al-
most believe it was a real
person being executed under
your eyes; I know the sight
just turned me sick with
horror.

And yet Li Sing himself
exercised a curious fascina-
tion over me for all that.

His delight in this hideous performance was so unmixed, and his face so impassive withal, while he gazed and gloated, that I couldn't help loitering behind after the rest had gone to have a bit of a talk with him. By way of facilitating the interchange of ideas, I gave him a dollar, which he pocketed at once with many fervent expressions of Oriental gratitude. I understood him to wish that my great-great-grand-father might be ennobled for this munificent deed, and that my remoter ancestors might each receive a step up in the table of precedence in their existing place of celestial residence.

"Melican gentleman lookee tired," Li Sing said, after a while, observing how I leaned on my stick for support. "Melican gentleman no wantee sittee?"

"I'm not an American," I said in reply. "I'm an Englishman, from over the sea, a stranger in San Francisco. But I shouldn't mind sitting down for a minute or two, if you've got a stool handy."

Li Sing looked at me hard ; after which (as it was almost closing time) he pushed Guiteau on his trial unceremoniously from his place, and handed me the chair in which the waxwork murderer had been peacefully seated. It was a very comfortable chair indeed, for a prisoner at the bar, and I sank into it most agreeably. " You no know nobody in Flisco, then, Englishman ? " he inquired with curiosity.

" No, nobody," I answered. " I'm just down on a visit. Not been long in America. I go back to-morrow. But I had an hour to spare this afternoon, and I didn't know what to do with it, so I just strolled in casually to see the waxworks."

79

Li Sing seemed interested. " Waxworks velly good," he said. " Guillotine velly good. Allee samee likee leally cut head off. English gentleman takee cup of tea? Waitee to see Li Sing clean up guillotine and puttee back head again ?"

It was a hateful sight, and yet I was very tired. And I was still English enough for the promise of a cup of tea to appeal to all the profoundest sentiments and sympathies of my nature. I nodded assent. I was distinctly sleepy. A cup of tea would help to wake me up. And then I must go down to the bureau once more and inquire whether they'd cabled the *Sacramento* yet.

Li Sing went off to fetch the tea and tea-pot. He was in high spirits for a Chinaman. He brewed the mixture under my eyes with a little spirit lamp. Of that

THAT

I was glad, for after what I'd seen of China Town the evening before, I rather suspected Chinese cleanliness. But nothing could be nicer or neater than Li Sing's five-o'clock-tea arrangements. He had a pretty little porcelain pot, and two dainty cups of Oriental red; and he poured out the liquor steaming, with cream and sugar as a concession to my western tastes; and I confess, better or more stimulating tea than that I never drank, and never shall, I fancy.

However, I was so drowsy even before I drank the tea that I could hardly keep my eyes open while he completed his arrangements. Once or twice, indeed, my head dropped back listlessly in Guiteau's chair; and once or twice I woke again with a start, to see myself confronted by Marat in his bath, with Charlotte Corday,

as pale as death, in the act
of sticking a cheap Pittsburg
knife into him. And after
the tea, strange to say, I felt
sleepier still; so sleepy, that
in less than ten minutes I'd
dozed off altogether, and was
conscious of nothing more
in the room around me, except a vague sense that I
was sleeping in the midst of
a conclave of murderers.

My sleep, however, wasn't
unbroken by appropriate
dreams. I slept heavily,
almost as if I had been
drugged; but I was dimly
conscious for all that, through
a haze of memory, of a sort
of hideous nightmare that
kept me strained and atten-
tive. I imagined I was a
slave on the middle passage.
My hands and feet were
bound with chains; my arms
were tied; somebody was
tugging away hard at the
fetters that clanked on my
ankles. A growing discom-
fort seemed to oppress my

82

limbs. I was sitting cramped in a row with a dozen others. But whiffs of China Town seemed to intervene as well. There was an odour as of opium; while the gangs of slaves on either hand were, not black, but yellow. And up and down through the human mass that thronged the stifling hold in which I gasped for breath, Li Sing, the Chinaman, moved bland and impassive, casting a phlegmatic glance to right and left as he paced the floor, and murmuring to himself in his broken pigeon English, "Good, good; velly good; makee plenty blood; makee plenty kill for Melican gentlemen."

CHAPTER VI.

THE JAWS OF DEATH IN REAL EARNEST.

"Shadows are trailing,
My heart is bewailing,
And tolling within
Like a funeral bell."
LONGFELLOW.

BY-AND-BY, I was aware of a trickling of water over my feverish brow, and a movement of air about my burning throat. I was gasping and ill: my tongue was dry, and my head aching. I opened my eyes slowly; I stared around me with a start. Li Sing was fanning me with a fan, and applying eau-de-Cologne to my aching forehead with a wet towel.

No more than that seemed

84

clear to me at first. I was merely aware of an unpleasant sensation of coming to, much as I have since felt it after having a tooth drawn under gas at a modern dentist's.

I raised my eyes feebly, and saw Lucrezia Borgia smiling down upon me from her sallow, pallid bust, and Mrs. Bates, the murderess, preparing to stab her sleeping victim. In a minute more, I remembered where I was, and recognized that for some hours at least I must have been sleeping heavily. It was pitch-dark without, and the Chamber of Horrors was lighted up within by a single kerosene lamp, which just sufficed to throw a ray of visible gloom upon the distorted faces of all those waxen murderers. A terrible fear seized upon me that the *Sacramento* might by this time have really come in, and that

85

Edith might have found herself, on her landing, alone
among strangers.

I put my hand into my
pocket to feel for my watch ;
or at least, I tried to ; but
to my utter surprise, I dis-
covered I couldn't move a
joint of my arm. Was this
rheumatism or paralysis ? I
gave a mad wrench. Great
heavens ! what could it
mean ? Ah, gentlemen, you
may stare. My arms and
legs were tied ! Tied with
a stout new rope, that con-
fined me to the chair. I
was bound hand and foot in
Guiteau's seat, unable to
move a muscle for my own
deliverance.

"What does this mean,
you scoundrel ?" I burst out,
the sense of my helplessness
just beginning to dawn upon
me. "How dare you at-
tempt——"

But before I could get
another word out, Li Sing
had stepped behind me

with dexterous rapidity, and quicker than I knew what was happening, slipped something adroitly into my mouth between my open teeth— something that prevented me from uttering a single cry or sound, and that no struggling on earth could ever avail me to get rid of. I recognized in a moment that it was a cunningly devised mechanical gag, with indiarubber adjustments, like those that are used for gagging the mouths of guillotined criminals. It formed part of the apparatus of that hideous show, and Li Sing had shown it to us the afternoon before with all the other paraphernalia of his hateful exhibition.

As soon as it was fitted on, and I sat there, helpless and speechless, but trembling all over with rage, Li Sing stepped back a couple of paces deliberately, and cast an admiring glance at his

HIS

own careful preparations.
"English gentleman, don't
be afraid," he said, in his
horrible jargon. "Li Sing
only tly little piecey expeliment. English gentleman
makee dollar present to Li
Sing. Li Sing go out buy
piecey lope while gentleman
sleepie, and tie up lope lound
English gentleman."

He smiled a bland smile
of infantile delight at his own
cleverness as he said it. But
his words appalled me. The
scoundrel had used my own
dollar that I gave him, to
buy the rope with which he
had bound me hand and foot
in the murderer's chair there.

Then it dawned upon me
slowly that he must have
hocussed my tea, and kept
me asleep there on purpose
while he bought the rope
and bound me.

I don't know whether the
Chinaman read this suspicion
in my angry eyes, but at any
rate he looked me back in the

88

face, and answered me almost as if I had spoken to him. "Yes, English gentleman," he said, gazing across at me pensively from those mild almond eyes of his, "Li Sing burn piecey opium in the loom while gentleman sit and wait for tea. Li Sing put piecey Indian hemp in tea-pot. Indian hemp velly good for makee gentleman sleep. Indian hemp bling plenty dleam. Li Sing go out and buy piecey lope to tie gentleman up while gentleman sleep there." And he laughed musically.

A cold thrill of horror coursed through my bones. I realized in a flash the full awfulness of the situation. The impassive, phlegmatic, pitiless yellow man had me wholly at his mercy, and could murder me, if he chose, with no more compunction than you or I would show at crushing a cockroach.

The very deliberateness

with which he spoke and moved had something inhuman in its crawling cruelty. He toyed with death as a cat toys with a mouse. He played with his victim, with a smile on his face, as a boy plays with a frog while he mangles it mercilessly.

I may be prejudiced, gentlemen, as I said before, but somehow, I can never quite trust those yellow-faced Chinamen.

Presently, he disappeared for a moment, and then came back with a bucket of water. He laid it by the side of the guillotine, and worked the knife up and down in the groove to see if it went smoothly without a hitch anywhere. After that, he sat down on a stool before me, like a man who has plenty of time to spare, and needn't hurry himself. I knew now he had awaked me and refreshed me with eau-de-Cologne in order that

he might enjoy the full
delight of watching my
helpless misery. He looked
at me close, not savagely,
but good-humouredly (which
was ten thousand times
worse), and smiled once more
that bland, infantile smile ;
" Li Sing workee guillotine
evelly day," he said slowly
and very distinctly, watching
my face as he spoke, to see
if it twitched ; " Li Sing
makee plenty blood flow ;
but never blood from living
Melican gentleman. Allec
time, Li Sing want to see
how guillotine workee on
living man. To-day, Eng-
lish gentleman come see Li
Sing; talkee Li Sing in
loom ; tellee Li Sing him
stlanger in Flisco. Li Sing
tinkee, this good time for tly
piecey expeliment. English
gentleman alone ; English
gentleman tired. Makee
English gentleman go sleepie
with Indian hemp in Gui-
teau's chair. Go out buy

lope, tie English gentleman up. Now go cut head off English gentleman."

The stolid joy of blood with which he spoke added to the horror and awe of my situation. In a moment, a ghastly picture rose up before my eyes. I thought of Edith, coming alone by night to that strange town, and finding when she arrived her future husband missing—perhaps even learning at once by what horrid fate he had died. For her sake, I fervently prayed one prayer. If Li Sing killed me, I trusted at least he would escape detection. I trusted he would destroy every trace of blood. I trusted his crime would never be dis-covered. I trusted Edith might never know the awful truth as to my disappearance.

Li Sing looked at me once more, and once more he smiled. He seemed to read my thoughts with Oriental cunning. "Melican judge never find out," he said, shaking his shaved head till the pigtail waved behind him. "Li Sing always buy bucket of blood evelly day in market. Plenty of blood in Li Sing's drain. Washee up allee right, makee guillotine clean again. Takee body to China Town, likee Chinaman do. Sendee box to China Town cemetelly with body to belley him. Chinaman no wantee know what body I belly. English gentleman stlanger in Flisco; got no flends. Nobody comee askee after English gentleman."

He told me all his vile scheme cynically, just so, with a chuckle of delight. Then he rubbed his hands quietly in passive Celestial joy. "Tly guillotine at last on live gentleman's neck," he said, hugging himself with the pleasure of an ideal achieved. "See plenty blood lun out; live blood; warm, beautiful!"

I groaned inwardly. It was all I could do. I was tied so tight from head to foot that I couldn't move a limb or a finger any way. And Edith by this time might be looking for me in vain at every hotel in San Francisco.

At last, after he had gloated long enough over my helpless condition, the Chinaman rose again, and came towards me cautiously. He cut with his knife the rope that bound me externally to the chair, and unwound it by stages. I could see then that he had used two pieces of rope, one to tie me rigidly from head to foot in a stiff, upright position, and the other to bind me to the chair, with cramped legs, while he made his final preparations for guillotining me.

As the outer rope was

94

loosed, I made one violent effort to shake myself free; but all in vain. Li Sing had done his work far too cleverly for that. He was a practised hand, for he had been an assistant in a hospital at Hong-Kong, he told me. I couldn't wriggle a limb half an inch either way under those firm close knots of his.

He lifted me in his arms, all rigid as I lay, and carried me over in his arms as one might carry a log of cordwood, for I had no more power of will or motion. Then he laid me down on the platform of the hideous machine, and fitted my neck into the horrible groove. I looked up, and saw the hateful knife gleaming over my head. Li Sing looked up too, and chuckled to himself audibly. "Plenty blood lun, lun," he said. "Velly plitty expeliment. Li Sing wantee allee time to see how guillotine workee on Melican gentleman."

No, gentlemen ; I tell you, it's not all prejudice.

The yellow man is as pitiless as Nature herself. He kills, and laughs. He tortures, and enjoys it.

Li Sing stood watching me with my head in the groove, in my helpless agony, for full five minutes. Evidently, now he had gained his heart's desire at last, he couldn't bear to get over the scene too quickly. He wanted to drink it in, bit by bit, and taste its full flavour by rolling it delicately on his mental palate. The five minutes seemed to me like a perfect eternity. But I knew they were no more, because he took out my watch, and held it up visibly before my eyes. I saw it pointed to twenty minutes past two in the morning. "Give you five minutes," the Chinaman said, with the watch in his hand. And then, he counted them out with deliberate slowness. " One . . . two . . . three . . . four . . . and a quarter . . . four and a half . . . four and three quarters . . . five ! And now for the expeliment !"

As he spoke, with stolid, fiendish joy gleaming childishly on his smooth face, he clutched at the cord, and gave a hasty pull to the weighted machinery. I closed my eyes, and knew all was up. I had but one last prayer : " Heaven grant that Edith may never learn it !"

How long a time a second seems when you're waiting for the axe of a guillotine to fall ! Slowly, slowly, the awful thing slipped down. I heard it slide in the groove with incredible deliberateness. I waited and wondered, with my eyes closed. But as the second lengthened itself out to half a minute at least—half an eternity, rather —I opened my eyes at last once more, and glanced patiently upward.

Li Sing stood gazing at the knife with a disappointed look. And the blade itself, which I had heard sliding slowly downward in its groove, and grating against the side, stuck in the machine half a yard above me.

This was unspeakable suspense, in the very jaws of death. Why torture me so by such delays? Was it chance that had done it, or was Li Sing still playing with me? Was he trying intentionally to prolong my agony?

But no. Something had surely gone wrong with the working of the machine. There was a hitch, clearly. Li Sing lifted the knife slowly into place once more, and examined the weights and pulleys with close atten-

tion. Then he slid it up
and down twice or thrice to
try it, and felt with his hand
for any obstruction in the
channelled groove. At last
he appeared to have found
it. He chuckled to himself
once more, and stood up on
the platform, gazing benignly
at the knife. All was ready
now for the final attempt.
At last my awful suspense
would be ended—by death ;
and in two minutes more I
should be free from a world
that grows such things as
these yellow-faced China-
men !

CHAPTER VII.

THE CHANCE OF A MINUTE.

> " The day is done, and the darkness
> Falls from the wings of Night,
> As a feather is wafted downward
> From an eagle in his flight."
> LONGFELLOW.

WHAT did he do then ? Well, then, gentlemen, he adjusted the weights, and put my neck back on the block neatly, for he'd kicked me aside for a time with his foot while he examined the machinery. He kicked me aside carelessly, as if I was a log of wood ; but it was hardly a moment to stand on ceremony, you'll admit, and I didn't insist. In fact, I could neither move nor speak, to remonstrate in any way.

But that wasn't just what I was going to tell you next. I've told this story so often now, I've got to tell it my own way, or I can't get through with it. You see, I've been leaving Edith rather in the lurch all this time, and natural politeness prompts one to return to the lady. Well, this is how matters fared with her while I was tied up. Of course I wasn't there to see it all myself; but I tell you as it was told to me afterwards.

About eight o'clock that night the *Sacramento* was telegraphed from the Farallone Islands; and Joe Ashley, who was still on duty at the bureau, awaiting the packet —sent up a little note at the Palace Hotel, where I was staying, and where he expected to find me on the look-out for Edith's arrival. Four hours later, almost as the clock was striking twelve, the vessel came to an anchor in the Golden Gate, and passengers were allowed to go ashore on the tender.

Now, it was part of Joe's duty, as it happened, to see the tender land her mails; so he was down on the wharf, by good luck, when Edith arrived there. If he hadn't been there, Heaven knows what might have happened. He recognized her the moment she came off the steamer—for he'd seen her photograph hanging up in my hut at Cooper's Pike here—so he touched his hat, and went up to her like a friend. "Miss Deverel, I believe?" says Joe.

And Edith nodded.

"Well, Mr. Freke's somewhere about on the look-out for you, miss," Joe said, politely, for he was always a gentleman. "Confounded odd thing he ain't here to the fore. He was up all night yesterday, waiting for you to arrive; and I sent him word to his hotel when the *Sacramento* was cabled from the Farallone Light, so he's sure to be loafing around somewhere on the wharf. But I don't see him. Jest you sit yourself down on this coil of rope, miss," Joe went on, looking around, " and I'll go up and find out if he's fallen asleep in the waiting-room. You see, he was up all last night waiting for the cable, so he's got a sort of an excuse for being sleepy this evening," Joe says apologetically. For he felt my remissness demanded an apology. He had a tender heart, Joe, and he was sorry for Edith. And I must admit that nothing but circumstances over which I had no control—such as being tied on my back under the axe of a guillotine by a bloodthirsty Chinaman— would ever have excused my absence from the post of duty at such a moment.

103

But circumstances, gentlemen, are sometimes too
many for the best of us.

As for poor Edith, she
felt naturally bewildered at
finding herself left alone,
this way, at twelve o'clock
at night, on an open wharf,
with a strange man, in a
foreign city. If she grum-
bled a bit at my faithless-
ness, I can't blame her very
much ; for you see, she
could have very little idea
indeed how precious little
control I had over those de-
taining circumstances. However, there she sat, a little
apart from the crowd, on a
coil of rope, watching every
one who passed with an
eager eye, and waiting in
vain for me to come and
fetch her.

For ten minutes or more
she waited there, shivering.
Here was a pretty welcome,
indeed, for an English bride
to the country where she'd
come to meet her future

husband ! At last Joe came
back, more bewildered than
ever. " I don't understand
this at all, miss," he said.
" It's a most astonishing
thing. Mr. Freke ain't anywhere about in the waiting-
rooms or saloon ; and I've
searched the whole wharf
without finding a trace of
him anyhow. This is darned
strange," Joe went on, looking sheepish himself at my
not turning up. " All I can
tell you is, he's been down
at the bureau of the Pacific
every hour for the last
twenty-four, a'most, to ask if
the *Sacramento* was cabled
from the Farallones ; and he
meant to come down as
punctual as clockwork the
moment she was due. I
can't make it out. It beats
me altogether where the
durned thing can have laid
himself."

" Oh, dear," cried Edith,
wringing her hands, and
looking over the edge of

the wharf, to where the lights were dancing on the ripples of the harbour; "you don't think he can have fallen into the water, do you?"

"No, I don't, miss," says Joe, very positive, just to quiet her mind a bit; for the suggestion gave him quite a start, it seemed so very probable. "But anyhow, we can't leave you sitting out like this till Mr. Freke turns up. I'll tell you what I'll do. I'll hire a hack and drive you up to your friends; and then I'll light out for Mr. Freke's hotel, and hunt him up, and bring him along to the house to see you."

"Oh, thank you," said Edith, feeling quite grateful to the man for his kindness, for she didn't know herself in the least what to do, and it was a comfort for her to have anybody at hand to advise her. Happily, it never even occurred to her innocent soul that he might be a crook—that's American for a pickpocket — or she might have been afraid to accept his escort. But she was too simple for that. She thought no evil. So Joe—he was always a good fellow, Joe was—he hired a hack, and saw her luggage safely aboard, and piloted her up to her friends' residence, on Jefferson Street, close to the Presidio Reservation. But as soon as he'd got her safely stowed away there—and of course, it took some time to get the hack and so forth — he hurried away at the top of his speed, with the very same horse, to the Palace Hotel, right down town on Montgomery Street.

For he was frightened a bit what had become of me, Joe was.

The moment he reached there, he rushed into the bureau. Now, I suppose you know the Palace Hotel is the biggest establishment of its sort in the United States, and they keep open all night, with electric lights burning; and when Joe looked at the clock, he saw it was just on the stroke of two, for it's a precious long drive from the Presidio to Montgomery.

"Hello, sir," says Joe, to the hotel clerk at the register, "has 1427, Mr. Freke, of England, been toting around this evening?"

The hotel clerk looked at the key, hung up on the peg, and shook his head. "Why, 1427 went out for a promenade at two o'clock this afternoon," he said, "and hasn't returned since. I guess he's making a night of it away down in China Town."

"By Jingo!" says Joe, growing pale. "It's worse than that, I'm afraid. Those blamed yellow men must have drugged him and robbed him."

"Very likely," says the hotel clerk, quite jauntily, going on with his books. "That's a common event. A most ordinary occurrence of life in China Town."

Well, when Joe heard that, he didn't stop to wait a moment longer. He ran as fast as a pair of Kentucky legs could carry him to the nearest police - station, and there he set what he knew before a cute Western inspector.

"When did you last see him?" says the inspector.

"Four o'clock," says Joe. "And then he told me he was going to the Metropolitan Plastographic."

"Halt there!" says the inspector. "That's the first thing to try. We've a clue, any way. There's a yellow-skinned Mongolian sleeps there to keep watch. I know the fellow well. Li

Sing's his name. If murder
and robbery's up, it's his
friends that have done it.
These fellows always belong
to a gang, I believe. Not
but what," says he, " Li
Sing's always been a solitary,
well-behaved sort of a chap.
But there ! you never know
where you are with these
yellow - skinned Mongo-
lians ! "

So off the inspector started,
with Joe in tow; and at
twenty-five past two by
the City Hall clock, they
were standing abreast of
the Metropolitan Plastographic.

And it was twenty-five
past two, as I dare say you
recollect, by my own watch,
when Li Sing let the knife
drop for the first time in
that infernal guillotine.

When they reached the
door, they looked about for
a bell. But there wasn't
any, it seemed. Then the
inspector said, " We'd better

not disturb the fellow at his game, perhaps. Let's go round to the back. He sleeps at the back, of course. Hello! What's up? Why, there's a light round yonder in the first-floor window!"

For the Chamber of Horrors, though on the ground floor from the front as you entered, was one floor up at the back of the house, the level of the street being raised somewhat above the natural surface.

"Let's climb up," says the inspector, "and see what's afloat. Perhaps we shall find them dividing the swag there."

Well, they both climbed up, and looked in at the window. The blind was down, but looking round the corner, through the chink of the sash, they could make out something. "Hello, this is odd." "This ain't anything at all," said the inspector; "I've seen Li Sing do all that a hundred times before. He's only arranging the machinery of that durned guillotine. Though he's chosen a most remarkable hour to do it in!"

"But what's that under it?" Joe said, looking closer. "That ain't the French king. . . . It ain't dressed up right. . . . That's not waxwork at all. . . . S'help me God, inspector, that's a living man the brute's got under it!"

At that precise moment, with a violent effort, I rolled myself over out of the way of the axe; and Li Sing turned sharp round to put me back on the block again.

Before he could do it, however, the inspector and Joe both gave a shriek of horror. In a second they had crashed through the glass of the window, and burst like thunder into the dim-lighted room. Li Sing turned round without a cry or a word. For one instant he faced them, imperturbable still, with that sphinx-like smile upon his Mongolian features. Then the full consequences of the discovery seemed to dawn upon him suddenly. He flung up his hands, and let go the weights. That moment the flashing knife descended with lightning-like rapidity down the grooves in my direction.

How it all happened next, I could hardly tell for a moment, for I was blinded with blood, and stunned with horror. But I felt at least my head was still there. Li Sing had been standing on the platform, adjusting the mechanism, and was stooping to replace my neck on the fatal block, at the very second when Joe and the inspector entered. As he flung up his arms and let the weights go, the knife descended, striking him on the flat of his back, and

knocking him down sense-
less on the platform above
me. The blood spurted out
from his broken spine, and
he gave one wild shriek.
But I myself was unhurt.
I was only terribly stunned
and shaken.

In three minutes, the in-
spector had cut away the
ropes, and lifted me from
the floor, and brought in
some brandy. Li Sing lay
writhing half insensible on
the platform. He wasn't
dead. He lingered on for
three days, indeed, and was
conscious at times; but for
the most part he lay delirious
on a bed at the hospital, and
merely muttered to himself
feebly from time to time,
" Plenty blood lun out. English gentleman stlanger in
Flisco. Li Sing only want
to tly piecey expeliment."
On the third day he died, in
fearful agonies. The injury
to his spine was quite irre-
parable. And it was better

so. If he had lived to be tried, the mob to a certainty would have caught him and lynched him.

Well, yes, of course, I was shaken a bit, no doubt. It was ten days before I was in a state to be married to Edith; and meanwhile, my hair turned white as snow. But Edith, when she saw it, fully accepted my apology for failing to meet her.

Why, certainly, I did my level best for Joe, of course.

He's now the secretary of the Cooper's Pike Natural Gas Supply Association.

Did you happen to notice that pleasant-looking gentleman in the yellow buggy, with the fast-trotting mare, that passed us with a nod this afternoon in the San Quentin Park?

Well, that's Joe, gentlemen. He's one of the most prominent citizens of Cooper's Pike at the present moment; and Edith and I

I sometimes think that when our Eustace grows up, and comes home from Harvard, he might do worse than make a match of it some day with Joe Ashley's Dolores.

THE END.

Jarrold and Sons, Printers, Norwich, Yarmouth, and London.

Jarrold & Sons' "Greenback" Series of Popular Novels

—CONTINUED.

In crown 8vo, cloth, 3s. 6d. each.

London: 10 & 11, *Warwick Lane, E.C.*

Jarrold & Sons' "Greenback" Series of Popular Novels

—CONTINUED.

In crown 8vo, cloth, 3s. 6d. each.

By *MRS. LEITH ADAMS.*

Bonnie Kate
Louis Draycott
Geoffrey Stirling
The Peyton Romance
Madelon Lemoine
A Garrison Romance

By *IZA DUFFUS HARDY.*

A New Othello!

By *SCOTT GRAHAM.*

The Golden Milestone
A Bolt from the Blue

By *T. W. SPEIGHT.*

The Heart of a Mystery
In the Dead of Night

By *MRS. H. MARTIN.*

Lindsay's Girl

By *E. M. DAVY.*

A Prince of Como

By *LINDA GARDINER.*

Mrs. Wylde

By *MRS. BAGOT HARTE.*

Wrongly Condemned

London: 10 & 11, Warwick Lane, E.C.

Jarrold & Sons
Series of Popular Novels

—CONTINUED.

In crown 8vo, cloth, 3s. 6d. each.

By *FERGUS HUME*.

The Lone Inn   [Court
The Mystery of Landy
The Mystery of a Han-
    som Cab
The Expedition of
    Captain Flick

By *LE VOLEUR*.

By Order of the Brother-
    hood !

By *JOHN SAUNDERS*.

A Noble Wife

By *E. BOYD BAYLY*.

Jonathan Merle
Alfreda Holme   [ture
Zachary Brough's Ven-
Forestwyk

By *EVELYN*
EVERETT GREEN.

St. Wynfrith and its
    Inmates

By *MRS. HAYCRAFT*.

Gildas Haven

By *HUDE MYDDLETON*.

Phœbe Deacon

London: 10 & 11, Warwick Lane, E.C.

www.ingramcontent.com/pod-product-compliance
Lightning Source LLC
Chambersburg PA
CBHW022142020726
47496CB00008B/2509